ISBN 1 85854 723 7
First published in Great Britain in 1998 by Brimax
This edition published in 2000 by Brimax
an imprint of Octopus Publishing Group Ltd
2-4 Heron Quays, London E14 4JP
© Octopus Publishing Group Ltd
Printed in Spain.

TODDLERS'
Bedtime Storybook

Illustrated by
Gill Guile

Contents

Tessa the Kitten

Tessa the kitten plays with a ball. She chases it across the floor, under the chairs and around the table. Sam the dog watches. He stops the ball with his paw. "Meow! Meow!" says Tessa. "Stop it! That is my ball!"

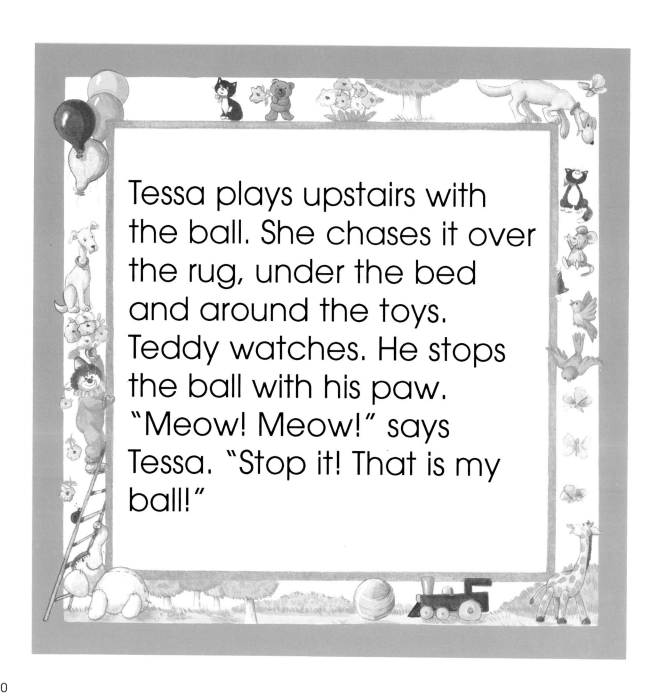

Tessa plays upstairs with the ball. She chases it over the rug, under the bed and around the toys. Teddy watches. He stops the ball with his paw. "Meow! Meow!" says Tessa. "Stop it! That is my ball!"

11

Tessa the kitten plays outside with the ball. She chases it over the grass, under the bushes and around the trees.
A bird watches. He pecks at the ball.
"Meow! Meow!" says Tessa. "Stop it! That is my ball!"

Tessa chases the ball
indoors and into the
kitchen. It bounces in her
saucer and splashes her
nose with milk.
"Atishoo! Atishoo! Stop it,
you naughty ball!" says
Tessa. "Meow! Meow!
Meow!"

15

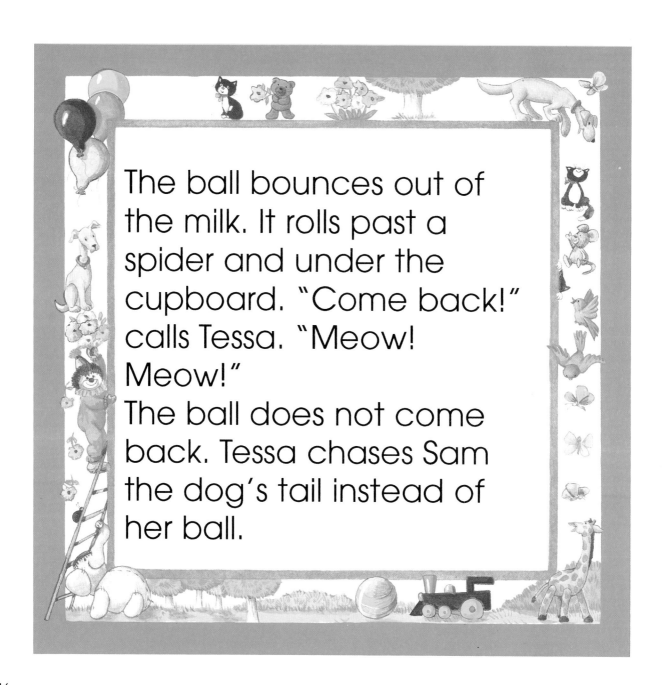

The ball bounces out of the milk. It rolls past a spider and under the cupboard. "Come back!" calls Tessa. "Meow! Meow!"

The ball does not come back. Tessa chases Sam the dog's tail instead of her ball.

17

"Woof! Woof!" says Sam.
"Please leave my tail
alone."
"I have lost my ball," says
Tessa. "I am sad. Meow!
Meow! Meow!"
"Do not cry," says Sam.
He shows Tessa a balloon
he has found. Tessa plays
with it.

The balloon bursts. BANG!
The noise makes Tessa
jump! "Meow! Meow!"
she says.
Now Tessa is tired.
She drinks her milk and
washes her paws. She
curls up beside Sam. Soon
she is fast asleep.

21

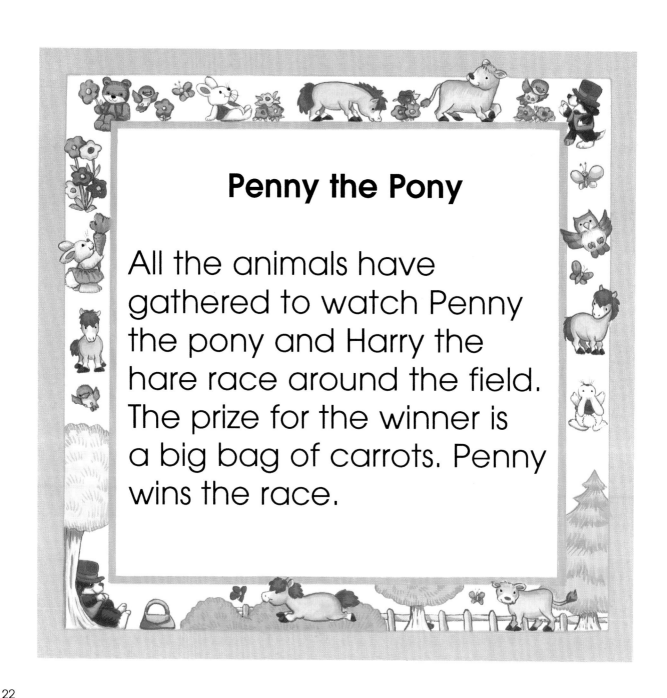

Penny the Pony

All the animals have
gathered to watch Penny
the pony and Harry the
hare race around the field.
The prize for the winner is
a big bag of carrots. Penny
wins the race.

23

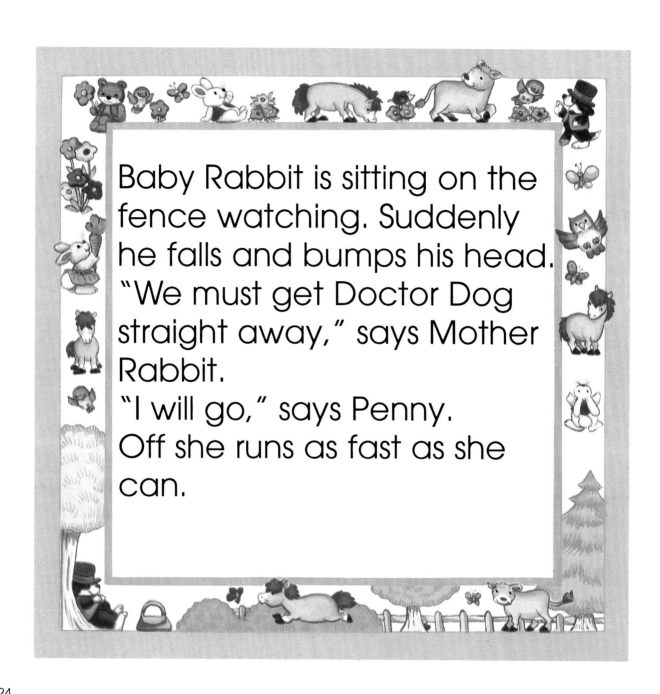

Baby Rabbit is sitting on the fence watching. Suddenly he falls and bumps his head. "We must get Doctor Dog straight away," says Mother Rabbit.

"I will go," says Penny.

Off she runs as fast as she can.

25

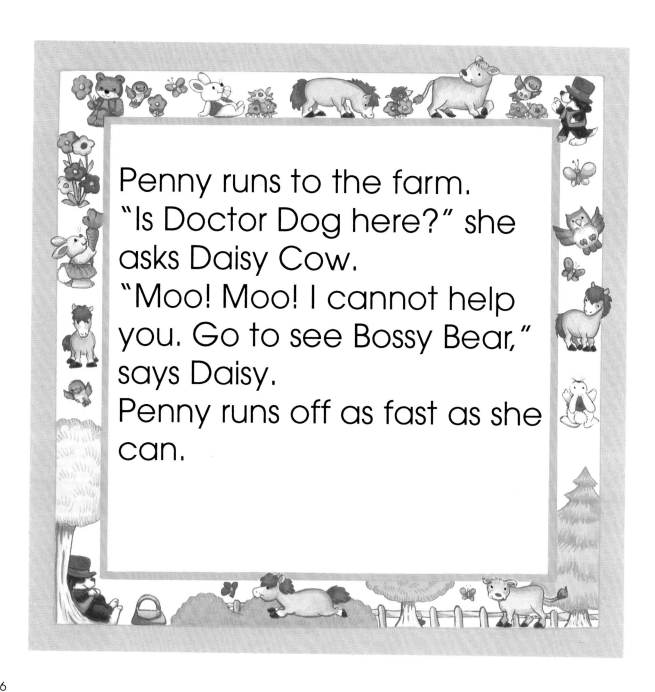

Penny runs to the farm.
"Is Doctor Dog here?" she
asks Daisy Cow.
"Moo! Moo! I cannot help
you. Go to see Bossy Bear,"
says Daisy.
Penny runs off as fast as she
can.

27

Bossy Bear is digging his garden.

"Where can I find Doctor Dog?" Penny asks him.

"Go to the wood and find Olly Owl. He knows everything," says Bossy.

Penny runs off as fast as she can.

29

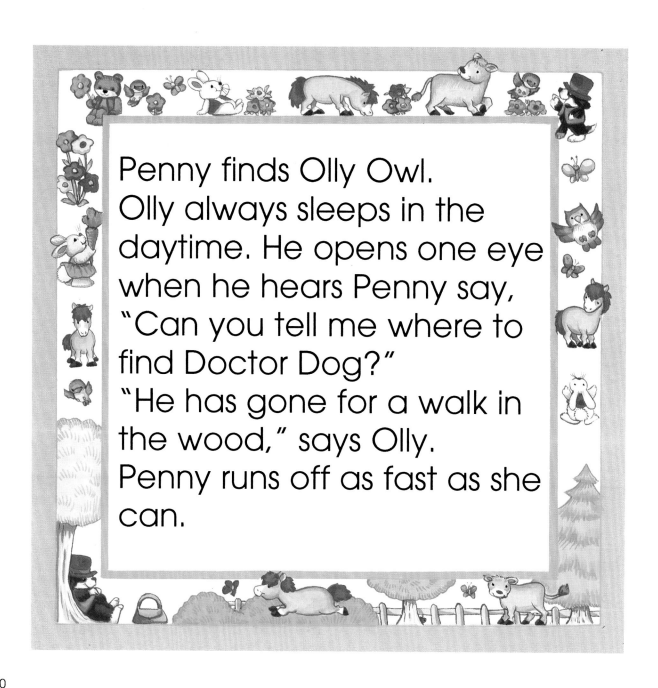

Penny finds Olly Owl.
Olly always sleeps in the daytime. He opens one eye when he hears Penny say, "Can you tell me where to find Doctor Dog?"
"He has gone for a walk in the wood," says Olly.
Penny runs off as fast as she can.

31

Penny catches up with Doctor Dog and tells him about poor Baby Rabbit. He jumps onto Penny's back. She gallops back to the field as fast as she can.

Doctor Dog looks at Baby Rabbit's head.
"There, there, all better now," says Doctor Dog.
"Thank you Doctor Dog and Penny the Pony," says Mother Rabbit.
But Penny has already gone to eat her carrots!

35

Three Little Ducklings

Bossy Bear's telephone rings.
It is Dilly Duck.
"It is the ducklings' surprise birthday party on Saturday," says Dilly. "Please call Paddy Dog and ask him to come."
"I will," says Bossy.

37

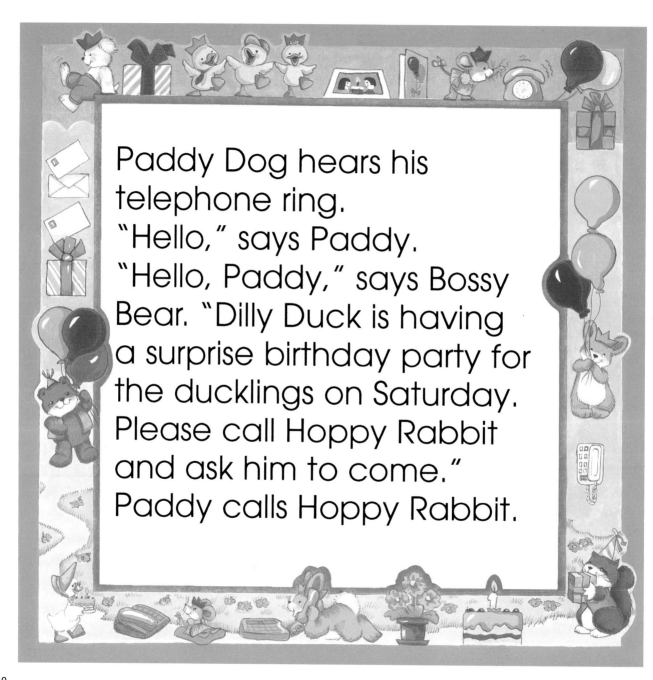

Paddy Dog hears his telephone ring.
"Hello," says Paddy.
"Hello, Paddy," says Bossy Bear. "Dilly Duck is having a surprise birthday party for the ducklings on Saturday. Please call Hoppy Rabbit and ask him to come."
Paddy calls Hoppy Rabbit.

39

Hoppy Rabbit's telephone rings.

"Hello," says Hoppy.

"Hello, Hoppy," says Paddy Dog. "Dilly Duck is having a surprise birthday party for the ducklings on Saturday. Please call Sammy Squirrel and let him know."

Hoppy calls Sammy Squirrel.

41

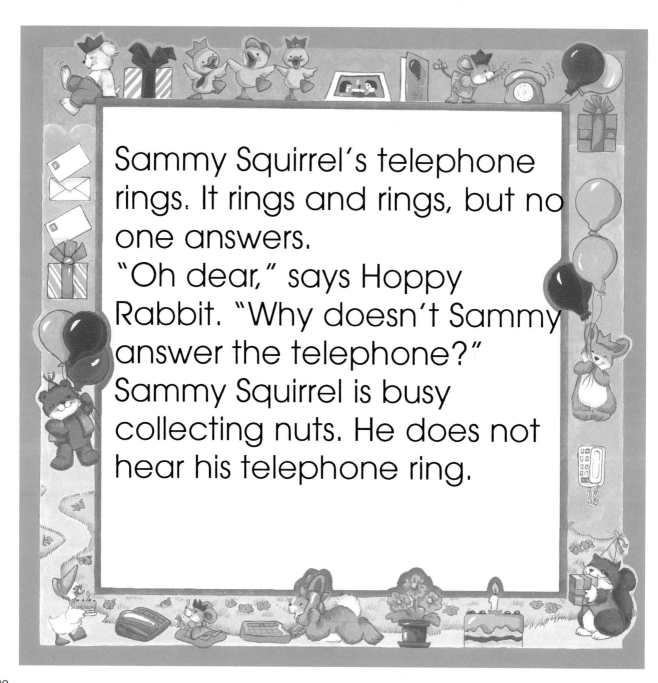

Sammy Squirrel's telephone rings. It rings and rings, but no one answers.

"Oh dear," says Hoppy Rabbit. "Why doesn't Sammy answer the telephone?"

Sammy Squirrel is busy collecting nuts. He does not hear his telephone ring.

43

Hoppy Rabbit goes to see Sammy Squirrel to tell him about the party. He finds him in the garden.
The telephone is ringing again.
"Why don't you answer your telephone?" asks Hoppy.
"You answer it," says Sammy.
"I am too busy."

45

Hoppy Rabbit answers the telephone. It is Molly Mouse. She has called Sammy for a chat. Hoppy says Sammy is too busy to talk. Hoppy tells Molly about the party. "What time does it start?" asks Molly.

"At three o'clock," says Hoppy.

47

It is Saturday. What a surprise the ducklings have when they see all their friends. The telephone rings. Dilly Duck answers it. It is Grandma.

"I'm on my way," says Grandma. When she arrives with the cake, they all sing happy birthday to the ducklings.

49

Cassie the Cow

Cassie the cow cannot find her calf. She calls for him. "Moo! Moo! Moo!" she says. There is no answer. Cassie starts to look for her calf. She passes Farmer Brown on his red tractor.

51

Then Cassie sees Paddy
Dog. He is chewing a bone.
"Have you seen my calf?"
asks Cassie.
"No I haven't," says Paddy.
Cassie is very upset.
"Moo! Moo!" she calls as
she walks towards the pond.

53

At the pond, Mother Duck
and her ducklings are
making lots of noise.
"Quack! Quack!" they say.
Cassie can see that her calf
isn't there.
"Moo! Moo! Where are
you?" calls Cassie.

55

Cassie goes to the pig sty. The piglets are squealing as they play in the mud. They are very dirty. Cassie sees that her calf isn't there. She hurries across the farmyard calling, "Moo! Moo! Where are you?"

57

Cassie sees Mother Hen.
She is very busy. She has six
fluffy chicks to look after.
"Have you seen my calf?"
asks Cassie.
"Cluck, cluck, no," says
Mother Hen.
Cassie calls for her calf.
"Moo! Moo! Where are
you?"

Cassie reaches the meadow. She can see the lambs and ponies playing. She looks carefully, and yes, she can see her calf there too!

"Moo! Moo!" she calls to him. She is happy and angry at the same time.

Cassie's calf hears his mother calling him. He runs over to her.

"You were very naughty not to tell me where you were going," says Cassie.

"I'm sorry," says the calf.

Then Cassie takes her baby home.

63

Little Lost Chick

Paddy dog and his friends find a baby chick crying in the woods.
"Are you lost?" asks Bossy Bear. The baby chick nods his head.
"Cheep! Cheep!" he says.

65

"Don't cry," says Dilly Duck.
"We will help you find your
mother."
"Do you know where you
live?" asks Hoppy Rabbit.
The little chick shakes his
head.
"Cheep! Cheep!" he says.

The animals look for Mother Hen. They look behind the trees. They look under the bushes. They cannot find her anywhere.

"Let's look by the pond," says Paddy Dog.

But the little chick still cries and shakes his head.

The animals look by the pond.
"Have you seen Mother Hen?" Dilly Duck asks her ducklings.
"Mother Hen is at the farm," they say.
The little chick nods his head and says, "Cheep! Cheep!"

71

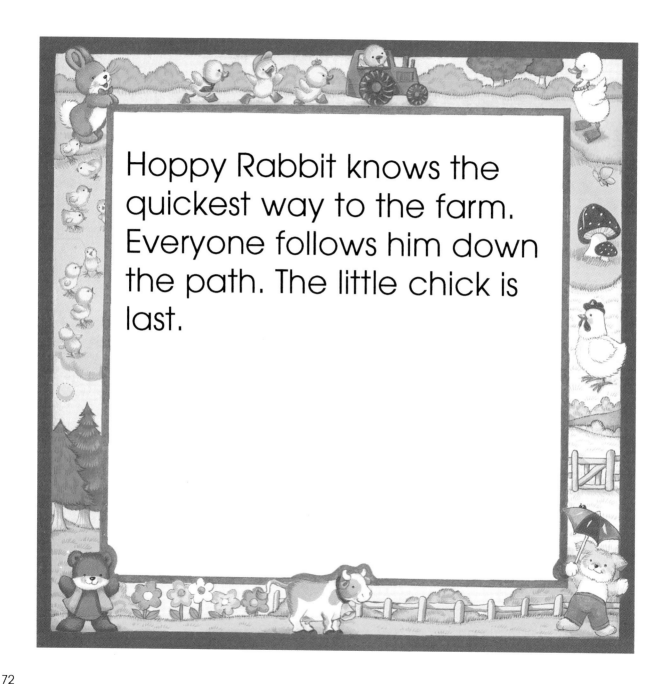

Hoppy Rabbit knows the quickest way to the farm. Everyone follows him down the path. The little chick is last.

73

"We are nearly there," says Hoppy. "Look! There's Gertrude the cow in the meadow."
The little chick knows that he is nearly home.
"Cheep! Cheep!" he says.

Mother Hen hears her chick and runs across the farmyard. The little chick is very happy to be home with all his brothers and sisters. "Thank you for bringing him home," says Mother Hen to Hoppy Rabbit and his friends.